# A
# LIFE

# A LIFE

Victor Feldman

Mary Guckian

*Dear Brief*
*Enjoy play*
*Best wishes,*
*Mary Guckian*

Swan Press

Swan Press,
32, Joy Street,
Dublin 4.

Copyright © with authors 2015

ISBN:   978-0-9560496-6-7

Art cover design by Christine Broe

Layout and Design L M N Dublin
liammcnevin@gmail.com

Printed by Johnswood Press. Dublin.

# Foreword

*'A Life'* took shape and form after having waded through, by chance, a mass of Mary's past poetry. They were almost diarist in their foot printing of Mary's past take on how life shapes us. I gradually after some long period fitted the pieces together in the hope of coming out with some coherent shape. As I wasn't around to record the actual past circumstances of how the shapes took place, the characters are possibly therefore shadows of shadows that I have strained to give some form of life to. And then just when the script was lying in an old attic gathering dust, by some odd chance as life often does luckily present us with. I managed to rope up a willing cast and the fruitful help of Ron Loughnane's gift of rehearsal space in his camera repair shop on Dame street. And then luckily enlist two highly talented actresses I had worked with in the past, Sarah Byrne and Joan Thorpe. As well as the highly esteemed actor Ron Loughnane. And then it was just a point of sewing all the various threads together to produce *'A Life'*.

Victor Feldman

January 20th 2015

# A LIFE by Victor Feldman with Poetry by Mary Guckian.

*For the reading of this radio type play have six actors sit on High stalls...have two telephones as props...and a wireless of the 70's period....The performance starts with the Narrator introducing the characters to the audience.........*

Narrator: Ladies and Gentlemen, if you could hush for a moment and possibly turn off your mobiles and assuming you know where the nearest loo's are, I'll then shed some light on the byways and flotsam that *A LIFE* might have unduly and possibly without warning taken hold of...... And so without further delay as life is, or was short enough without me wasting it any further. We'll go visit some of the possible misfits you might bump up against at the till in Smiths hardware or on the upstairs of the Seven bus into town, such as the ever present.

*FRANK:* Jenny's boyfriend…

*JENNY:* the rural dreamer and poet

as well as her rural *MAMMY:*

not to mention the other woman *CATHY:*

and the office runner *TONY:*

also the birthday girl *MARY:*

And the rest of the general flotsam of *LIFE* will

be played by the angels! Or namely me!

The *NARRATOR*…..


Ladies and Gentlemen, we present *A LIFE* by
Victor Feldman with poetry by Mary Guckian.
So sit back and imagine it's 1970's Dublin in
Jenny's sparse bedsit.  Late night folksy music
can be heard being played on an old battered
wireless as Jenny appears to be busy watching the
milk boiling on the cooker.  And also so it appears
preparing for her long bewildering nightcap…

Jenny :    This woman needs some visible body liner to
           soften her starved soul. *FLIP!* This milk is boiled
           over!  Allow me one shagging cup of cocoa,
           minus the aggro…

Narrator:  The phone intrudes from another planet. Maybe
           another time.  An echoing fate.
           Rrrrrrrrrrrrrrr! *(The sound of a phone ringing)*

Jenny:     Yes! *(pause)* Hello *(pause)* HELLO!

Mother:    It's Mammy.

Jenny:     Mammy are you well?  Did you take the
           laxatives…

Mother:    Jenny, when are you coming home?  There's
           some lambing and the...

Jenny:     In a week or so…

Mother:    Would ye get me those chest tablets ye were telling me of. Missus Kelly, you know! Who sweeps for the priest. The one married to Paddy who likes the flutter. Well, she's complaining badly of her chest. Wheezing the phlegm. I told her about the tablets anyway and...

Jenny:    I'll get them Mammy.. Is your chest alright?

Mother:    My Chest! It's fine. Why?

Jenny:    You're due up here in Dublin for the appointment soon.

Mother:    I am?

Jenny:    I'll collect you here at the station.

Mother:    That'll be good so!

Jenny:    Did you see Dinny Feely on the Late Late Show on the TELEVISION?

Mother: I did so. He looked fed. Enjoying himself…

Jenny: Do you remember his mam playing the banjo in Keely's bar across from the Mass.

Mother: She did? By the way, there's a Mass being said for Miss Kerrigan's granddaddy, when ye're home next so!

Jenny: Who?

Mother: Her who was always cribbing about the eggs… ach! She wouldn't know her hen from her duck!

Jenny: Did he die?

Mother: Who?

Jenny: The grandaddy?

Mother: About two years ago. The poor man. He used to jig down at the buttery.

Jenny:      LOOK MAMMY! I better go to bed now.  So bless you.

Mother:     And the Lord be to ye…

Jenny:      GOOD NIGHT MAMMY

Mother:     GOOD….

Narrator:   Before Mammy could utter another blurb Jenny near exhausted with words placed back the receiver and gulped down the last of her nightly cap.

Jenny:      FECK!  Where's my lover man?  Sinking into his last black and sagging home…

Narrator:    Jenny turned on the radio.

Radio:      That concludes our entertainment for tonight. And do please take note that next Sunday's scheduled Mass will be from the Church of the Blessed St. Anthony and not as was scheduled from the Blessed St. Oliver.  We do apologise for any inconvenience you parishioners in Ballycran might have suffered. But I'm sure your prayers

will still nevertheless be of joy.  I hope you have enjoyed tonight's entertaining schedule.
And don't forget to put out the cat before turning in.  OICHE MAITH! *(Good night)*

Narrator:    Jenny unplugged the radio announcer…

Jenny:    Bring in the cat! Did I ever leave him out?  The mangie rattle snake!  Face it Jenny my girl.  He would have rung by now.  The shite!

Narrator:    Jenny in a tide of yawns unrobed her soul, revealing her chiffon night clothes.

Jenny:    Jesus!  Where did I leave the hot water bottle..? where to settle before the storm…

Narrator:    A flushing lavatory beat crashed her thoughts as she picked up her hairy teddy.

Jenny:    No Teddy.  You'll never fill what my heart craves for.

Narrator:    She wound down the alarm clock to move from the bleak dark to another blight.

Jenny:     Now Jenny.  Remember you've been warned
           twice this month for time keeping.
           So be alert and scrubbed.  Late running repairs
           can be fine-tuned in the loo.  Leave your
           scribbles on the shelf until tonight.  It'll restore
           your sanity in some odd form or shape.  Lights
           off and deep passionate dreams pass me on to
           Cupid's shadow..

Narrator:  Jenny fell instantly into a long deep dreamland...

Jenny:     I want to share my life with you.
           To love and care about all you do.
           When emptiness comes across our paths
           I'll be waiting to enter in.
           Turn to me when all else fails
           I'll try and share what's left of me.
           It may not be much, it's very little
           Compared to life about us both,
           But, I admit I need you too.
           Don't hesitate, I'll be waiting.
           I'm forever there, can we try again
           Mould our lives together,
           And make a better place for both of us,
           Despite our ups and downs, it's
           Not the same without you being around.

Life here on earth is only short,
And loneliness is killing me fast,
So phone me now
Before it's too late
And in a lover's knot
We'll try again to heal
Our differences and love a lot.
I need your arms around me now.
This emptiness is wearing me.
I've loved life all along,
But once I shared I realise
On my own it is worth nothing.
I'm here waiting
To cling to you again.
I must not be selfish
It is only this earth
We are passing through
So here I am in bits
Willing to share
The part that is left
Before it's too late....

Narrator:     Suddenly the crashing din of a tsunami broke the
tidal wave as Jenny's ears were blighted with the
furious din of the morning alarm to arms…
*(sound of alarm clock ringing…)*

Jenny:     CHRIST! It's eight thirty.  Where's my undies
           and bra…?

Narrator:  Jenny scuttled to get dressed…

Jenny:     How do I look?  Mirror, mirror on the wall. No!
           Please don't…

Narrator:  The sound of her footsteps flew down the stairs
           and into the bathroom. She then stared wistfully
           into its mirror.

Jenny:     Oh odorous body cleaner. Lightening eye liner.
           Rescue me from this rat infested blight.  Salvage
           my last vestige of beauty.. before…

Narrator:  The ominous phone added to her blight.
           *(Phone ringing)*

Jenny:     Yes!

Narrator:  The lover!

Frank:     Jenny

Jenny:     WHAT?

Frank: Look Jenny, about last night. I'm really sorry but I got held up by one of the lads and then would you believe it I bumped into Brendan, you know the one with the legs. Well, how can I explain...

Jenny: Frank! Forget it. Right!
*(Jenny slams down the phone)*

Frank: Jenny, I can…

Narrator: Jenny then exhaustedly slipped into her Mini-Minor car, turned on the ignition and pulled out into the traffic amid the congestion and fumes of the city, her crisis revealing a plaintive cry…

Jenny: I'm a grown woman,
Just thirty three
Part of the world,
With feelings and
Passions as strong
As can be, loving
Each day, waiting
To see what it can
Bring, suffering
And sorrow.
Joys of tomorrow.

But waiting to live
And keep going
On music and excitement
To raise the pressures
Off the mind, free
The brain and see clearer
If life is nearer to death
To love, or must we
Just tread on.

Narrator:  As if the deities had screamed abuse enough…
her stream of consciousness was jolted by the car
radio news…

Radio:  'The woman's body was found near a field. The
police report stated that she was sexually
assaulted'

Jenny:  Spare me, oh Lord!

Narrator:  Jenny blotted the dark news with a turn of the
switch… before finally arriving at her work.
The constant rattle of typist and chat permeated
the office, blotting out all that we suffer… She
after staring into the abyss parked herself in front
of a typewriter.

Jenny: This lump of lead has me tied and gagged. Driving me to near exhaustion. Am I destined to sacrifice all to the great design? Forty years to the pension. I must search for kindred spirits… but then is it all really worth it? Yes! I'll fit in with the great design. What else is there?

Narrator: Ring! Ring *(phone rings)*

Jenny: Morgan's and Harris…

Frank: Jenny!

Jenny: YES Frank!

Frank: Look! I've two tickets for Lady Windermere's fan at the Olympia. It's by Oscar eh!...

Jenny: Wilde!

Frank: Mastermind babe!

Jenny: He's parked on my book shelf next to your empty beer cans.

Frank: Up against boozy Behan…

Jenny: Well then, Great Gatsby. I rescued him from your off license beer mats…

Frank:      LOOK JENNY, we can discuss conflicts in
            Mulligans after the play. I'll pick you up around
            six. You can reheat that Chinese curry I left in
            the fridge. And finish off the Chardonnay we
            opened last Sunday. You know the one we…

Jenny:      FRANK! See you tonight… let's enjoy the
            weekend!

Frank:      Look forward to seeing you.

Jenny:      Same old tune... try improving your repertoire
            of fine wit or should I say…

Narrator:   About to place back the phone…

Jenny:      Shit!

Frank:      Look Jenny…

Jenny:      Byeeeeeeeeeee! *(Jenny slams down the phone)*

Narrator:   Jenny slammed down the phone to the
            office chorus. (*The office blight bites back*)

Office      *HAVE YOU THAT INVOICE JENNY?*
Voices:     *CHECK THE BATTERLY'S OF*
            *BASINGSTOKE' 'THE COFFEE MACHINE'S*

*BROKEN DOWN AGAIN GET TONY TO FIX*
*THE DAMN THING'*

Narrator    The sound of office bedlam faded as she found herself with Frank in the audience of the Olympia Theatre at the famous play. The joy of Wilde's play breezed steadily by up to its final intoxicating words .......

Narrator:   Lord Augustus.

Voice:    'Miss Evelyn has done me the honour of accepting my hand'

Narrator:   Lady Windermere.

Voice:    'Well. You are certainly marrying a very clever woman'

Narrator:   Amid the grand applause of the final curtain Jenny and Frank hurried from the theatre to the grind of the street din, almost drowning their chatter.

Frank:    It wasn't that bad really! Not what I expected, but....

Jenny:    I've seen better productions…

Frank:     How about a drink then?

Jenny:     Straight from the script!

Frank:     No sense straying from the plot... just one!

Jenny:     Well...

Frank:     AH! Would you believe it... look over there! The palatial splendour of Bloom's hostelry. Leopold drank there many a night.

Jenny:     Just one then! How much was the ticket Frank?

Frank:     My treat. So you enjoyed the play then.

Narrator:  They meandered across through the traffic

Jenny:     It was a bit slow in the first, but it took off in the second...

Narrator:  They entered to the noisy din of the noted Dublin pub and grabbed two nearby stalls.

Jenny:     You see who played Lady Carlisle?

Frank:     No, whom?

Jenny:     Mary Gidney. Her brother worked with me in the Sligo courthouse. Always showing off her Raleigh bike. She'd lock it bang outside the court.

Frank:     A PINT, JOE,  AND A SHERRY…

Narrator:  Frank, shouted over to the over stressed barman.

Jenny:     Her older sister used to get Mammy her ailments.

Frank:     Was the actress a Sligo woman?  I've seen her somewhere.

Jenny:     Carrickfergus.  Her brother used to run the local poetry group.

Narrator:  A loss of words erupted as barman Joe placed the drinks down on the table, winking at Frank… Frank then sipped the ritual froth from the stout's silky surface.

Frank:     Mind you, the costumes were incredible.

Jenny:     The black gown Lady Plymdale wore reminded me of a dress I bought in Oxford…

Frank:     The period Jenny spent jobbing at the
           university…chasing writers.

Jenny:     I still have it in Mammy's home.  The black
           pearls at the base…*(A bell is heard ringing)*

Narrator:  Last orders.  Drink up!

Jenny:     Swallow down that drink Frank.  I'll get a fresh
           Chinese on the way home.

Frank:     LOOK!  Just a word with Joe.

Narrator:  While over at the bar..

Frank:     Joe, be a mate.  Give us a refill…

Joe:       Sorry Frank, drink up…

Narrator:  Frank headed back to the fold.

Frank:     Would you believe it?  The scrapes I got that
           facker out of…

Jenny:     FRANK! You've really drunk your fill.  And
           anyway we still have the Chardonnay to finish.

Frank:     BUT…

Jenny:     Please Frank, give it a break!

Frank:     I know you have a point and I understand, but…

Jenny:     If it's a problem FRANK…

Narrator:  He's slightly inebriated.

Frank:     It's nothing Jenny I can't handle. That's why I
           love you. Because that's why you…

Jenny:     Good! It's relieving to know we can handle it.
           Come on, let's get going!

Narrator:  The two of them having now squeezed the broom
           handle out of Life's constant struggle made the
           bus route to Jenny's mini bedsit, clustered in
           among the city's flatland. They finally, after
           climbing four flights of stairs, exhaustedly
           entered her nest.

Frank:     Anything on the idiot box?

Jenny:     We could catch the end of the Arts review…

put your feet up.  The curry's nicely done.

Narrator:  Jenny turned around to dish out the Chinese
and to her woe!!!

Jenny:  Ah No!  I don't believe it.  He's…

Frank:  Snorrrrrrrrrrrrrr!!!

Jenny:  Yes, with you it is easier
So I write while you pick up
the Chinese meal
On our way from Lady Windermere's Fan
The play was wit and humour
By that man Oscar Wilde
About his life of many years ago.
I'll tell you now
You bring love to life
Make it real for me.
You make up for living that was missed
And you take me from the stresses and struggles
In today's world of depressing office scenes.
I'll enjoy the meal with you now and always
Hold your hands when nights are frosty
And the meal will stay warm
Until we drive back to my room
To be together for another night.

Frank:      Snooorrrrrrrrrrrrrr!

Narrator:   Jenny slipped a warm blanket over him to allow
            him fill his dreams.

Jenny:      Good night my wonderful intoxicated slob.  See
            you in the morning.

Narrator:   The trusted and by now battered alarm clock
            again repeated its dawn chorus
            *(sound of the alarm clock ringing)*

Frank:      I DON'T BELIEVE IT! TEN PAST NINE!

Narrator:    He rose from the battered and worn couch.

Frank:      SOD IT!  She's gone!

Narrator:   A note lay leaning against the empty chardonnay

Frank:      Ah!  One of her love notes...

Narrator:   He reads its contents.

Jenny:      Dearest darling Frank, left you a hardboiled egg
            in the pot.  See you tonight at Mary's Twenty
            First in the Brazen Head as agreed.  I've penned
            a few jobs in the paper.  Take a look.

Love, Jenny. Kiss.

Frank:      OH SHITE! I forgot about the Brazen. The head isn't in gear these days. Must get to the Labour by eleven. HELL! BETTER MOVE! Shite! The phone…

Narrator:    Ringgggggggggg! The phone
*(sound of phone ringing)*

Cathy:      Jenny!

Frank:      Frank!

Cathy:      (*Whispering*) It's Cathy!

Frank:      She's gone to work.

Cathy:      I'll call her at the office.

Frank:      I really enjoyed your poetry at the Writers' last week…

Cathy:      Why, thank you Frank. Your comments were really kind. Why don't you write yourself?

Frank:      Jenny likes me to be there for a bit of moral

support.  You know.  Stop her from slipping over the edge.

Cathy:     Yes, I understand.  Her work is a bit over compassionate.  It's nice.  Very sweet.  Rural I suppose…

Frank:     Yes, now you say so it does.

Cathy:     I heard you were both at Lady Windermere's Fan last night.  Did you enjoy it?

Frank:     It was alright!  The bar was a bit squashed.  Still, it was a great evening.

Cathy:     Look Frank, I really must go.  But if you're passing by, don't be shy.  Pop in.  I'm usually at home most afternoons.  You could peruse my poetry.  Comments wouldn't go astray.

Frank:     I might just hold you to that Cathy.  OK, see you then.

Narrator:  He placed back the phone.  The day darkened as all humanity in all its shapes and weird forms struggles to keep tabs on all that life throws at it.  And as such Jenny having spent her day taking a hold in the race, struggled back into the bedsit to adjust to Frank's composite needs.

Jenny:     Did you have an interesting day?

Frank:     I collected the Labour.  Went over to the union. Nothing doing except in three months West Litho might interview me for the nights.

Jenny:     Great!

Frank:     That just about reflects my day.  Oh! I had a chance meeting with Donal.

Jenny:     DRINK!

Frank:     Look!  He invited me to discuss a new venture he's dreamed up.

Jenny:     THE MAGIC BOTTLE OPENER!

Frank:     On the button!  It's patented.  You see, it's like this…

Narrator:  Frank's a dreamer.  Jenny's a realist.  Where do you draw the line.  That evening the party at the Brazen Head went with a swing… 'The Huckle

29

Buck' moved the dancers... Except for Frank
and Jenny who chose to snigger alone in a far
off corner of the pub. The party girl, Mary, made
a feeble attempt to move them from their cosy
boredom..,

Mary:      Having a good time Jenny?

Jenny:     Terrific Mary,  lovely party.

Mary:      Help yourself to the cocktail sausages. Cheer up
           Frank.

Frank:     What?

Mary:      Smile!

Narrator:  Mary, the birthday girl, was whisked off by a
           passing male for a dance.  A pair of drinks were
           parked in front of them.  Slow smoochie dance
           music whiffed across the floor as Frank and
           Jenny stared into the dark shadows....

Jenny:     You've brought me this far
           And kept my sanity to date
           Despite my wasteful years.

Now I can live without upsetting you
And all the many people that I know
For I've learned to accept me as I am
And keep my stresses under control
To live and know life has many reasons
For giving us the nerve to cope.
If you care to live with me
I'll make no demands on you,
We'll keep our communication going
To trail that link that now we've found
And enjoy the pleasure of our desires
Keeping us in constant touch with life and love
And the reason for our meeting.
When life is low our desires bring forth
Pain and Suffering,
With you they seem to fade away
When I have you within reach.


Frank:   That was a lovely smooth pint.  Nice head on it.

Jenny:   Do you mind Frank if we go.  The din is really
          annoying me.  I've had to endure endless hassle
          at the office all day.. and…

Frank:   Jenny, we've only arrived.  We really should
          stay a while longer.

We can't be rude and just leave.

Jenny: So you can fill your head with a belly of black lather. I've really taken as much as I can. You really are the limit. Am I to pay for your drink all night? In fact am I to pay for your drink every night? I'm not a bottomless bank.

Frank: That's it! Jesus! Thank God we're not married.

Jenny: OH! THANK YOU! Wait! Mary's coming this way…. Hi Mary!

Mary: You two having a ball!

Frank: UNBELIEVABLE MARY!

Jenny: The pork pies are crazy.

Mary: Oh! Thank you Jenny. Jenny, you might like to meet Harry and Gerry over by the bar. They're both poets. They both know your poetry, love it they said.

Jenny: I'd just love to meet them Mary.

Mary: Come on over and I'll introduce you to them.

Jenny: I won't be long Frank. Here, I'll order you a

pint. Would you pay sweetie. I'm a bit short of change.

Frank:      Yea, sure!

Narrator:   The continued thumping beat of the disco repertoire rolled on, animating the dancers with the party swing. Jenny, suddenly animated, moved off to her two admirers. Frank, seizing the moment to capitalize on other possible gains whispered over to the oppressed barman…

Frank:      JOE!

JOE:        What the fack!

Frank:      Is there a phone around here?

JOE:        Over there near the gents.

Narrator:   He picked up the phone and…

Frank:      Cathy, it's me, Frank.

Cathy:      Hello Frank.

Frank:      Look Cathy, it just struck me that I have to pass by your place tomorrow. As my Auntie Mildred needs some ointment.  If it's alright with you I'll pop in for a while.  That is if you....

Cathy: Of course Frank, it's no problem.  Feel welcome. How is Jenny?  I didn't see her at the writers last week.

Frank: She's in great form Cath, eh! Cathy!  She often discusses your poetry.

Cathy: All constructive jibes accepted!

Frank: Ah, you know!  Jenny's all PC

Narrator: Jenny escaping the two poets headed back towards Frank.

Frank: Look!  She's heading back this way

Cathy: Tell her I love her poetry, except the verse…

Frank: See you tomorrow… byeeeee!

Jenny: Who was on the phone?

Frank: The phone?  Just a buddy.

Jenny: Mary has really good contacts.

Frank:      Really!

Jenny:      See that man sipping the cocktail over by
            Mary's mate……

Frank:      The baldy one!

Jenny:      He's assistant secretary to Rollins publishers
            over by the quays.  He's looking forward to
            reading my poetry.

Frank:      Well, don't let an insignificant little cod like me
            hold you back.

Jenny:      FRANK! What's in that drink?

Frank:      Ha!

Jenny:      Look, let's get going.  You really are not
            swinging with the flow….

Frank:      Yea!  Let's go.

Jenny:      Frank, I'm really sorry.  I've been a bit stressed
            lately.  My mother's been worrying me and…

Frank:      What is there to forgive?

Jenny:      Come on then, let's go.

Narrator: As Frank moved over to his bar pals, Jenny
stood outside in the street alcove facing the cold.

Jenny: It's so good
To find you in the night
To sit and talk for hours
On end, to get communication
Going and strike a chord of
Understanding. I'm happy
To chat and drink and talk
My mind to you, to share out
Ups and downs and relax
Among the crowds,
With noise all about.
I feel safe with you
And wouldn't swap you for
Anyone. Don't walk out on
Me at the end of the night,
Like many have done, but
Stay around and keep me happy.
Get me through the weekend, so
I can face another week
Of ups and downs.

Narrator: The following day the treadmill of the office
jargon penetrated the air... all life having been

there in all its myriad forms.

Office: *'GET ME THE MEMO FOR THE*
*TEASDALE FILE.....Jenny!*
*Have a detailed list of Stanmore project by*
*eleven.....If my wife calls, tell her I'll be home*
*around ten tonight'*
*RINGGGGGGGGGGGGG*
*(Sound of phone ringing)*

Narrator: The phone.

Jenny: Morgan's...... FRANK!

Frank: It's me.

Jenny: Frank! I'm up to my ears. ...

*Office jargon ........*

Office: *'Jenny... the meeting is being brought forward*
*by ten minutes.... the French delegation are due*
*in the boardroom...we'll need info on their*
*current demands... by this afternoon...Jenny is*
*that blasted coffee machine working?'*

Jenny: *(whispers........)*
I'll phone you back in a moment.

Frank:      JENNY!

Jenny:      FRANK! Can't this wait until tonight?

Frank:      NO!  It cannot.

Jenny:      What is so important Frank?  I cannot talk from
            here.  Say what you have to say and then we'll
            discuss it tonight.

Narrator:   Such were the chasms of life!

Jenny:      WELL!

Frank:      I think we should part the waves…

Jenny:      The what!

Frank:      Call it off!  We love each other but it just
            doesn't..

Narrator:   The phone as a sycamore glided down to its
            eternal Saviour… leaving Jenny to ponder as she
            slowly placed back the phone on its grateful
            receiver.

Jenny:    I knew it should never have happened
I never thought it would
When you decided you'd had enough
You know I always loved you,
And that I still do,
That your life with me
Was all I needed.
But to you it seems past
And gone. Here I am a
Lonely woman, broken hearted
Torn in bits, passing days
That are unending and
Struggling with the memories
Of a man I loved too much.
Trying to cope with feelings
And emotions in a body that
Had grown to know a love of
Tender feeling that will
Never go away.
As I try to keep my sanity
I'll never regret any moment
Of your company.
I know it is hard
To find a love
So deep so understanding.
And life is but a passing

Tide, finding its strength
keeping mind to hold
A body's sanity everyday.
I'll keep hoping that I'll
Find my needs elsewhere,
Even though it will never
Be the same. I'll go on.
Loving you every day.

Narrator: The sudden sharp shrill sounds of secretaries
screamed… the walls caving in… the contagion
of overheated rads…activated Jenny to claw at
the locked office window as a fish breaking from
its doomed tank. And then a call from above!...
*(rrrrrr!)*

Mother: Jenny, ye are near thirty four and no sign of a
man in your life. Sure ye have never been short
of offers. Look at Padraig with his draper's on
the best spot on the main street… And he still
speaking fondly of ye. His sister Bridget passed
away two years ago. And he alone now by
himself. With no woman to do his cooking,
scrubbing or cleaning. And he crying out for
a decent woman. And what in the name of St.
Anthony were ye doing with that Jackeen? Mary

Kelly heard many the story about that fellow. Modesty wouldn't allow me to repeat the woman's words. But I know Jenny, ye are a decent girl. And there's always a good clean room here. The cross of Blessed Ignatius is still above the bed. And your grannie's beads draped over the holy cross... Padraig's still waiting and praying. Father Kelly keeps watch. We're all here on our knees hoping and praying...

Narrator: The pestilence then compounded the blight!
The eternal phone. *(Ringgggggggg!)*

Frank: Look Jenny please try to understand. I'm really fond of you. Surely you realise that. We've been an item now for six years. In fact if it wasn't for my three month marriage debacle we'd have gone down the usual route. Think about it!

Jenny: We'd have crossed that line somewhere.

Frank: Jenny the eternal dreamer...be realistic for once.

Jenny: Now Cathy can refuel your empty beer cans.
Keep you afloat.

Frank: Now Jenny there's no need for that talk.

Jenny:      I will always love you Frank.  But we as you
            want must let go!

Frank:      There's no need to be harsh Jenny.  We can be
            adults or idiots…

Jenny:      You just tread your path and I'll lead mine…

Frank:      BUT!...Jenny But nothing…You are acting
            irresponsible Jenny…

Narrator:   The poor innocent phone. Once more as in a
            lovers tiff takes the rap… to the applause of the
            office.

Jenny:      (*she slams down the phone…*)

Voices:     '*Reilly and Son needs confirmation in ten
            minutes…Jenny call my wife and tell her I
            won't be home until late. Wish little Harry a
            happy birthday*'…

Jenny:      LORD GIVE ME A BREAK BEFORE

Narrator:   The blight appears… each unforgiving… each a
            a distant, shadow…

Mother:     Jenny are ye coming home this weekend?

Father Kelly is having an early Mass for Agnes Doyle. We're all aching for ye to return.

Frank:    Cathy and I intermingle with a love, secure in the space she gives me…

Jenny:    Paying your drink bills…

Frank:    I take comfort in the peace Cathy provides.

Jenny:    Financing you from the hunger. Shielding you from the storm…

Cathy:    He's handcuffed to my existence Jenny…

Mother:   Come home Jenny, Padraig is praying and hoping.

Jenny:    Give me strength!

Mother:   I've the kettle on and the treacle cake cut.

Cathy:    What have you to offer Jenny, but your fantasies…

Jenny:    You crush my dreams…

Cathy:    Scribble your verse…

| | |
|---|---|
| Office: | *Is that blasted coffee brewing… the Leydon account should have arrived… what's with it…* |
| Mother: | Sister Bernadette was over last week for tea… she had great craic in Lourdes… and left some holy water near your bed… |
| Jenny: | *(SCREAMS)* |
| Cathy: | He's mine Jenny… MINE! |
| Mother: | Padraig's waiting until he can wait no longer… |
| Voice: | *(Radio anouncer)* And don't forget to put the cat out. |
| Office: | *The coffee machine… coffee machine… machineeeeeeeee!* |
| Jenny: | OH! Hi TONY… |
| Tony: | Are you sure you're all right Jenny? Can I… |
| Jenny: | TONY! I couldn't be… couldn't be… couldn't be…finer. I just need… |

Tony:     Yes!

Office:   *TONY! Slip out and post the Magdalene dockets…*

Jenny:    It's just that…
          Back in my room
          Almost three weeks
          Of this emptiness.
          Now that I've rid
          Myself of you
          Is it right that we are
          Friends and polite
          One another.
          No more touching,
          Or taking your hand
          Linking in the street
          Putting my hand in yours
          When I stop the car
          At the traffic lights
          You don't have to worry
          About loose hairs making
          A pattern on your navy wool coat.
          No rows about the programmes
          To watch on TV or what we'll
          Have for supper,

What time to get to bed
Or a comforting embrace
When we lie in one another's
Arms in the single bed.
The peaceful times are gone.
Even if I'm glad to be rid
Of the traumas and emotions,
To get things right between us
Your tooth brush in the bathroom
Reminding me you're not there.
Yet, I'm unable to dispose of it in the bin.
Your photographs around the mirror
In my bedroom, look down on me,
As I try to read before falling asleep
In the early morning, and all seems
Peaceful with the world, hiding
So much of the truth we have to live with.
How long can I live with the silence?
Or is that what we both should do?
I know we can talk to one another
About all sorts of daily problems
And leave our personal ones out of reach.
I'm sitting here in front of the gas fire,
Lonely, with having you in the room.
But safely away from those emotions
That cause so many problems

And yet –
As I look around this room
And pack away the contents,
My mind jumps back to the time
We travelled and shared
The beauty of so many places.
That first picture I snapped of you
On the bridge of St. Stephen's Green
Is covered in dust, your bald spot
Seems darker than it is today.
The piece of pottery you made
At the workshop in the winter
Evenings is rough and thick lipped.
Your first attempt to try and capture
The pots and dishes you admired
In museums where we walked
Around together, often used before
The age of enamel, tin and plastic.
The card you gave me for my birthday
One June month, a copy of a painting
That I enjoy 'A Summer's Day'
By William Kay Blacklock, eighteen seventy…
I almost feel I could be that girl reading
Under a tree with a thatched house
In the background. A dog created
From sea shells by artistic hands

A work of art. The perfumed piece of delph
Still freshens my room, despite a passing
Year, I have that Toblerone chocolate cover
You brought along the evening I had a cold
And lay sick in bed, the bites of sweetness
Giving me new life.  The photograph
From our visit to Clonmacnoise on the way
Back from Cobh and your brother's wedding
The day before.  We both look distant
In our gaze, I was so upset then, a memory
I prefer not to know but try to understand
That we are all complex creatures
Of this universe, surviving in our own way.
The tape recorder, one of your last presents
Keeps me busy now recording and playing back
Some tapes you gave me.
Having so many memories that keep
You alive-alive-alive-alive.


Office:    *Jenny, have you the files for Morris and Sons…?*
             *Fax the accounts department*
             *WHERE'S THE BLOODY COFFEE…?*
             *IS TONY BACK…?*
             *WHERE'S TONY?*


Narrator:   THE END…………